TRANSFORMERS: DEFIANCE
ISSUE NUMBER THREE (OF FOUR)

WRITTEN BY: **CHRIS MOWRY**
PENCILS BY: **DON FIGUEROA**
COLORS BY: **JOSH PEREZ**
LETTERS BY: **CHRIS MOWRY**
EDITS BY: **DENTON J. TIPTON & ANDY SCHMIDT**

MEGATRON leads his army into space to destroy a battle group of aliens determined to capture the ALLSPARK. The fight is vicious and MEGATRON has protected CYBERTRON once more. But now that he has began speaking with a mysterious entity with ties to the planet's past, will MEGATRON continue to protect? Or will those that oppose him be punished? Meanwhile, PROWL and JAZZ have been asked to help OPTIMUS find an answer to why MEGATRON has suddenly become so brutal.

Special thanks to Hasbro's Aaron Archer, Michael Kelly, Amie Lozanski, Val Roca, Ed Lane, Michael Provost, Erin Hillman, Samantha Lomow, and Michael Verrecchia for their invaluable assistance.

To discuss this issue of *Transformers*, join the IDW Insiders, or to check out exclusive Web offers, check out our site:

 Licensed by: **DREAMWORKS** **PICTURES** **GM** OFFICIAL LICENSED PRODUCT

WWW.IDWPUBLISHING.COM

VISIT US AT
www.abdopublishing.com

Reinforced library bound edition published in 2010 by Spotlight, a division of the ABDO Group, 8000 West 78th Street, Edina, Minnesota 55439. Published by agreement with IDW Publishing. www.idwpublishing.com

Printed in the United States of America, Melrose Park, Illinois.
102009
012010
 PRINTED ON RECYCLED PAPER

Library of Congress Cataloging-in-Publication Data

Mowry, Chris.
  Defiance / written by Chris Mowry ; pencils by Dan Khanna, Andrew Griffith, & Don Figueroa inks by Andrew Griffith & John Wycough ; colors by Josh Perez ; letters by Chris Mowry.
     v. cm.
  "Transformers, revenge of the fallen, offical movie prequel."
  ISBN 978-1-59961-721-3 (vol. 1) -- ISBN 978-1-59961-722-0 (vol. 2)
  ISBN 978-1-59961-723-7 (vol. 3) -- ISBN 978-1-59961-724-4 (vol. 4)
  1. Graphic novels. I. Transformers, revenge of the fallen (Motion picture) II. Title.
  PZ7.7.M69De 2010
  741.5'973--dc22

                          2009036394

All Spotlight books have reinforced library bindings and are manufactured in the United States of America.

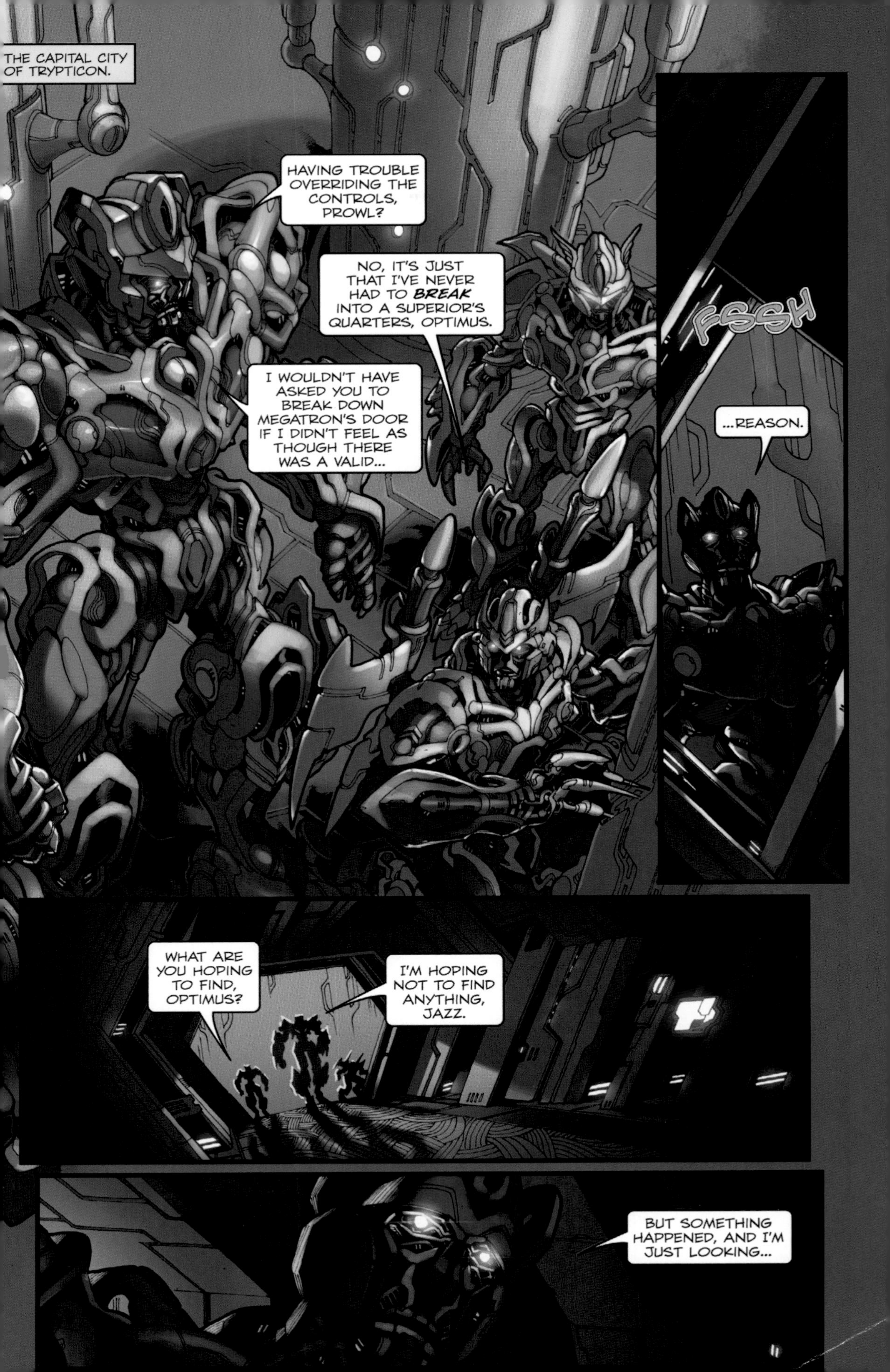
THE CAPITAL CITY OF TRYPTICON.
HAVING TROUBLE OVERRIDING THE CONTROLS, PROWL?
NO, IT'S JUST THAT I'VE NEVER HAD TO BREAK INTO A SUPERIOR'S QUARTERS, OPTIMUS.
I WOULDN'T HAVE ASKED YOU TO BREAK DOWN MEGATRON'S DOOR IF I DIDN'T FEEL AS THOUGH THERE WAS A VALID...
FSSH
...REASON.
WHAT ARE YOU HOPING TO FIND, OPTIMUS?
I'M HOPING NOT TO FIND ANYTHING, JAZZ.
BUT SOMETHING HAPPENED, AND I'M JUST LOOKING...

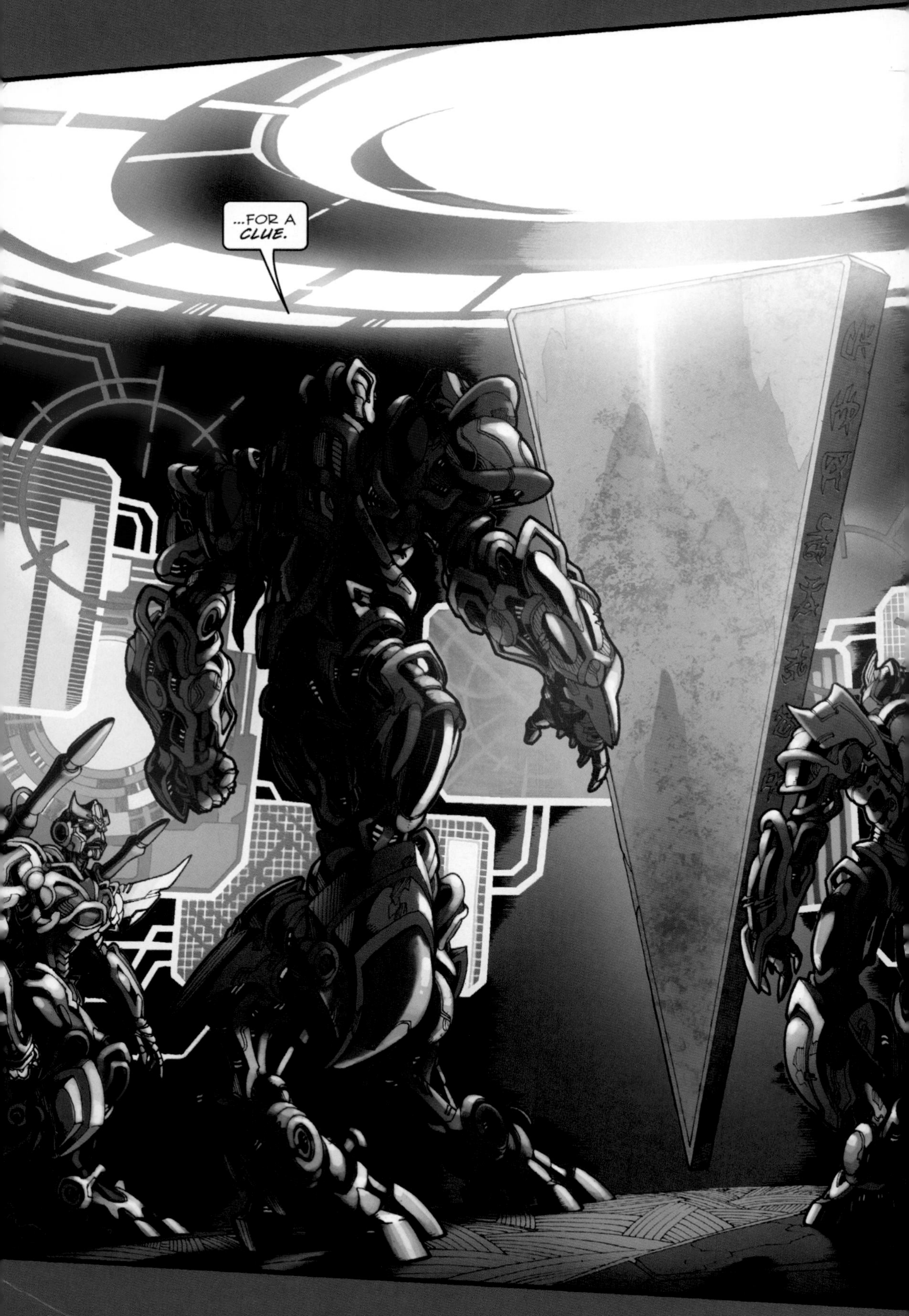
...FOR A CLUE.

FASCINATING, YET VERY CONFUSING.

WHAT DO YOU MEAN?

THE CONDITION OF THIS ARTIFACT WAS NOWHERE NEAR THIS WHEN IT WAS BROUGHT HERE. MEGATRON MUST HAVE CLEANED IT UP.

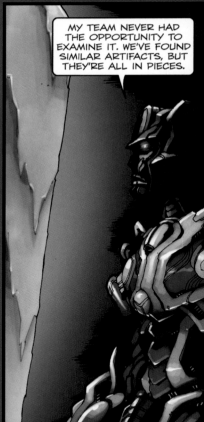

MY TEAM NEVER HAD THE OPPORTUNITY TO EXAMINE IT. WE'VE FOUND SIMILAR ARTIFACTS, BUT THEY'RE ALL IN PIECES.

YET THIS ONE SURVIVED. BUT HOW, OR WHY?

OPTIMUS! TIME'S UP!

SKYBLAST REPORTS THE BATTLE IS OVER AND MEGATRON IS ON HIS WAY BACK HERE.

VERY WELL, PROWL. I JUST WISH WE HAD MORE TIME.

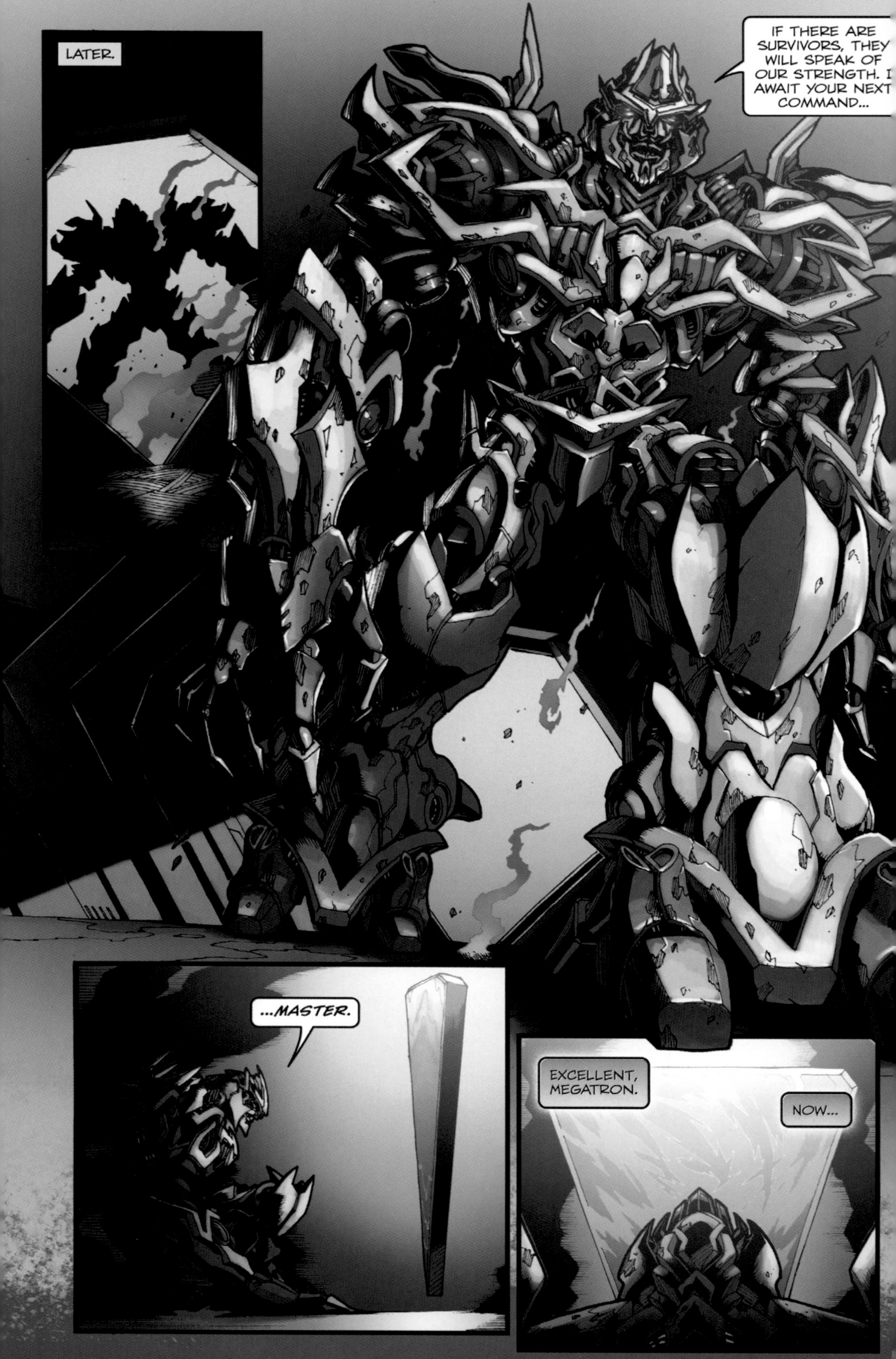

LATER.
IF THERE ARE SURVIVORS, THEY WILL SPEAK OF OUR STRENGTH. I AWAIT YOUR NEXT COMMAND...
...MASTER.
EXCELLENT, MEGATRON.
NOW...

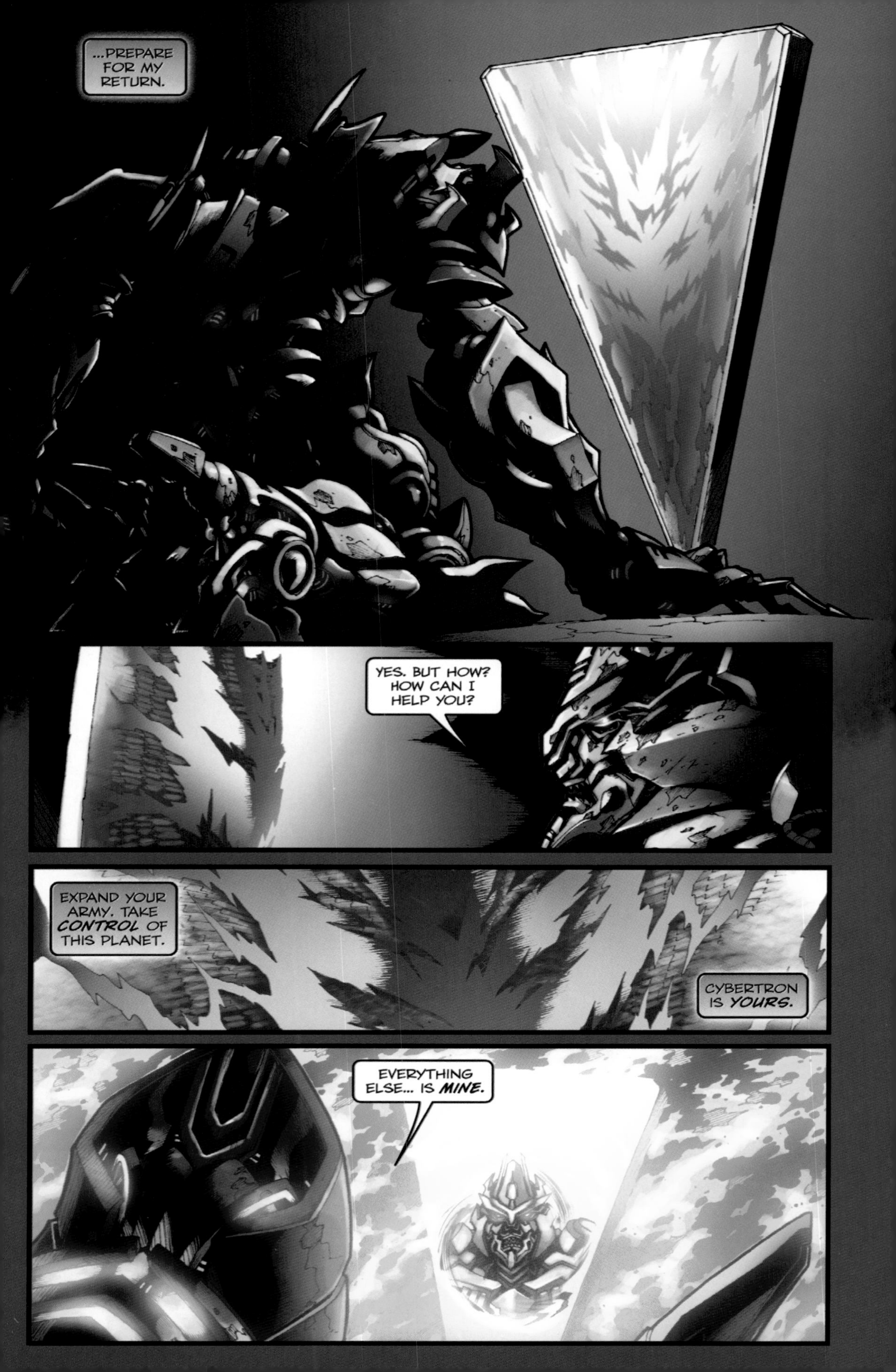
...PREPARE FOR MY RETURN.
YES. BUT HOW? HOW CAN I HELP YOU?
EXPAND YOUR ARMY. TAKE CONTROL OF THIS PLANET.
CYBERTRON IS YOURS.
EVERYTHING ELSE... IS MINE.

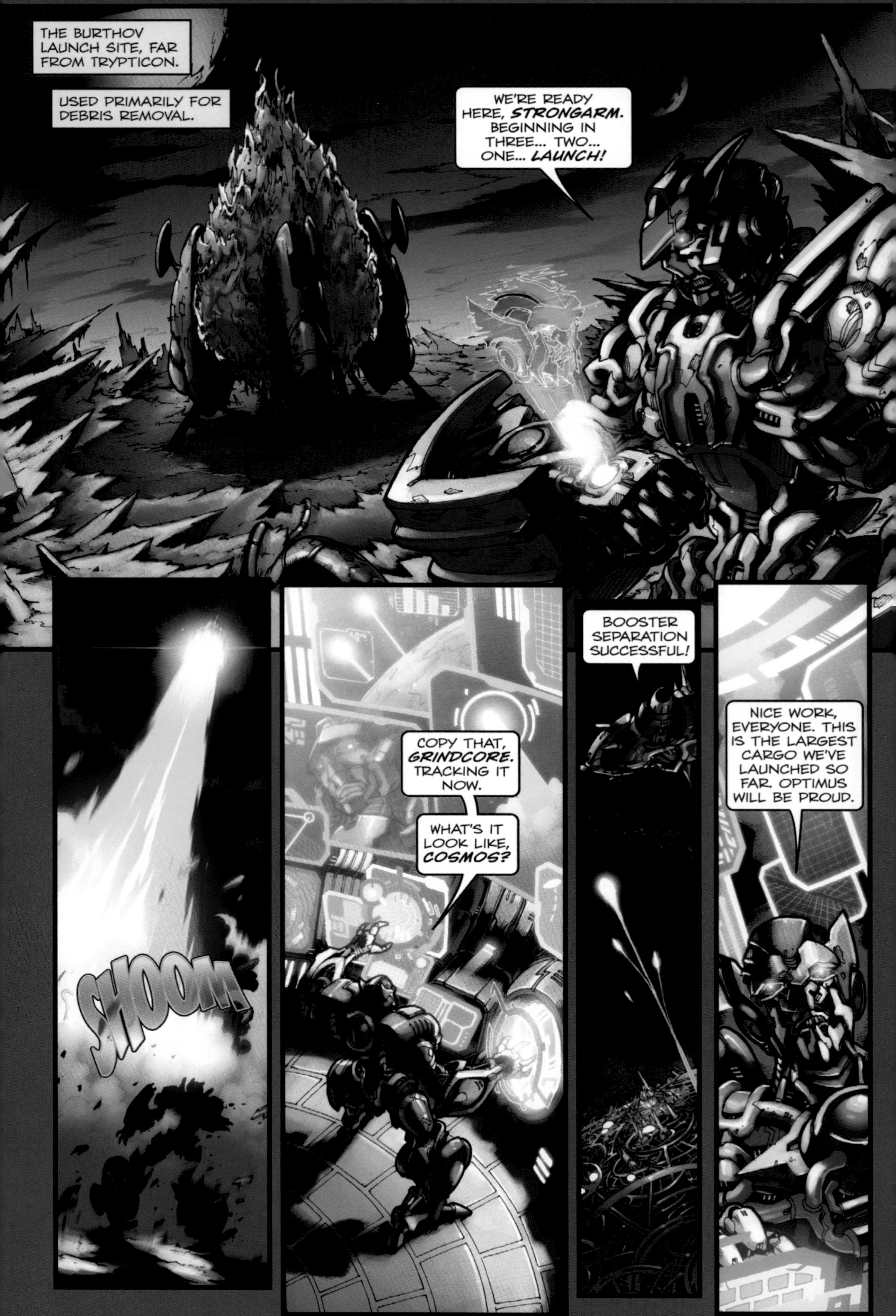
THE BURTHOV LAUNCH SITE, FAR FROM TRYPTICON.
USED PRIMARILY FOR DEBRIS REMOVAL.
WE'RE READY HERE, STRONGARM. BEGINNING IN THREE... TWO... ONE... LAUNCH!
SHOOM!
COPY THAT, GRINDCORE. TRACKING IT NOW.
WHAT'S IT LOOK LIKE, COSMOS?
BOOSTER SEPARATION SUCCESSFUL!
NICE WORK, EVERYONE. THIS IS THE LARGEST CARGO WE'VE LAUNCHED SO FAR. OPTIMUS WILL BE PROUD.

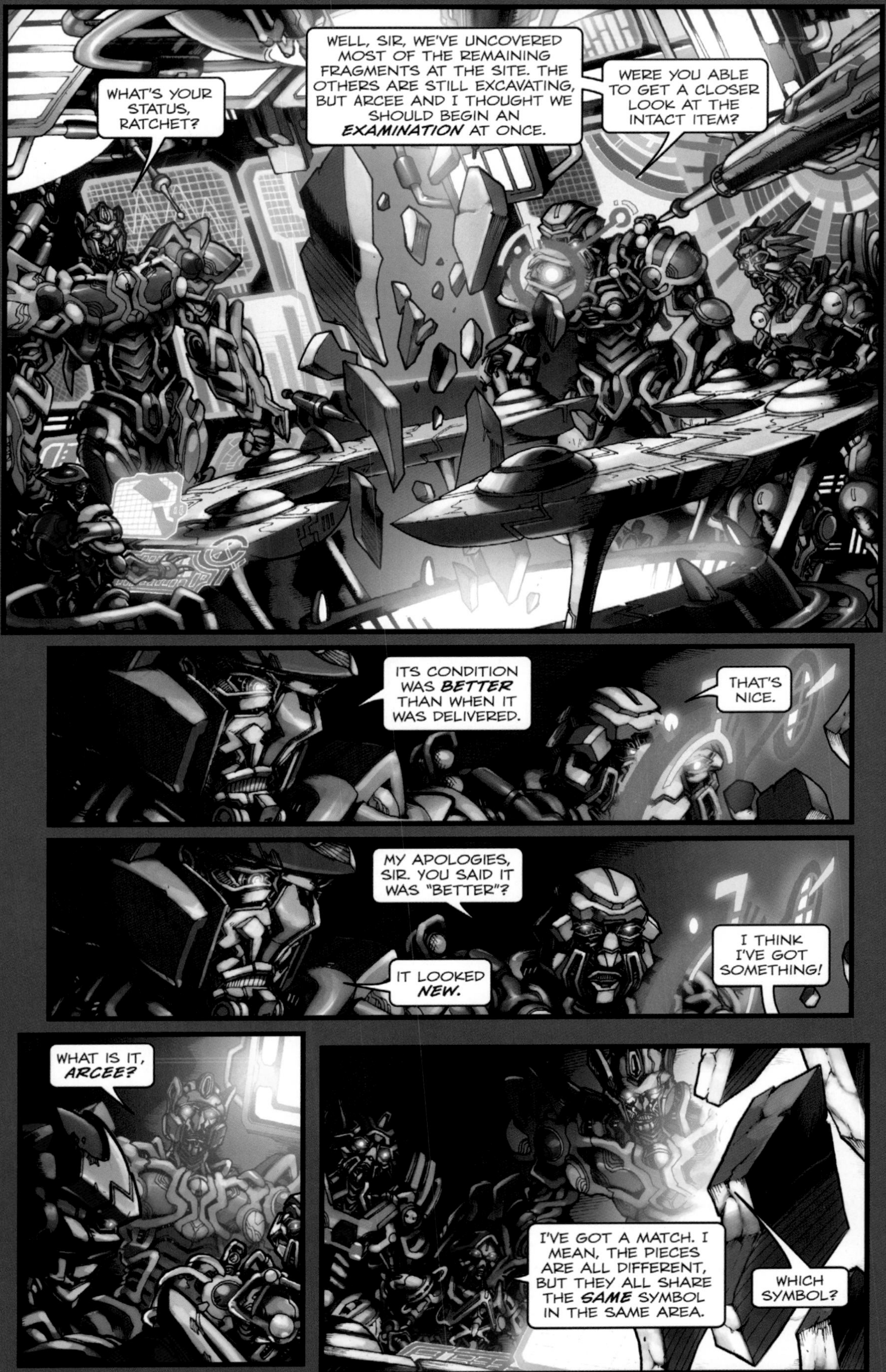
WHAT'S YOUR STATUS, RATCHET?
WELL, SIR, WE'VE UNCOVERED MOST OF THE REMAINING FRAGMENTS AT THE SITE. THE OTHERS ARE STILL EXCAVATING, BUT ARCEE AND I THOUGHT WE SHOULD BEGIN AN *EXAMINATION* AT ONCE.
WERE YOU ABLE TO GET A CLOSER LOOK AT THE INTACT ITEM?
ITS CONDITION WAS *BETTER* THAN WHEN IT WAS DELIVERED.
THAT'S NICE.
MY APOLOGIES, SIR. YOU SAID IT WAS "BETTER"?
IT LOOKED *NEW.*
I THINK I'VE GOT SOMETHING!
WHAT IS IT, *ARCEE?*
I'VE GOT A MATCH. I MEAN, THE PIECES ARE ALL DIFFERENT, BUT THEY ALL SHARE THE *SAME* SYMBOL IN THE SAME AREA.
WHICH SYMBOL?

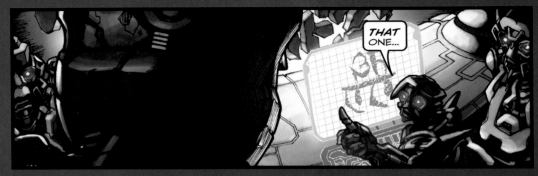

THAT ONE...

...ON *YOUR* HEAD.

OPTIMUS, THIS IS PROOF THAT THE *DYNASTY OF PRIMES* IS REAL!

AND AS HARD AS IT MAY BE TO ACCEPT, YOU'RE SOMEHOW *CONNECTED*...

"CONNECTED"? YOU MEAN I MIGHT BE...

...A *PRIME*?

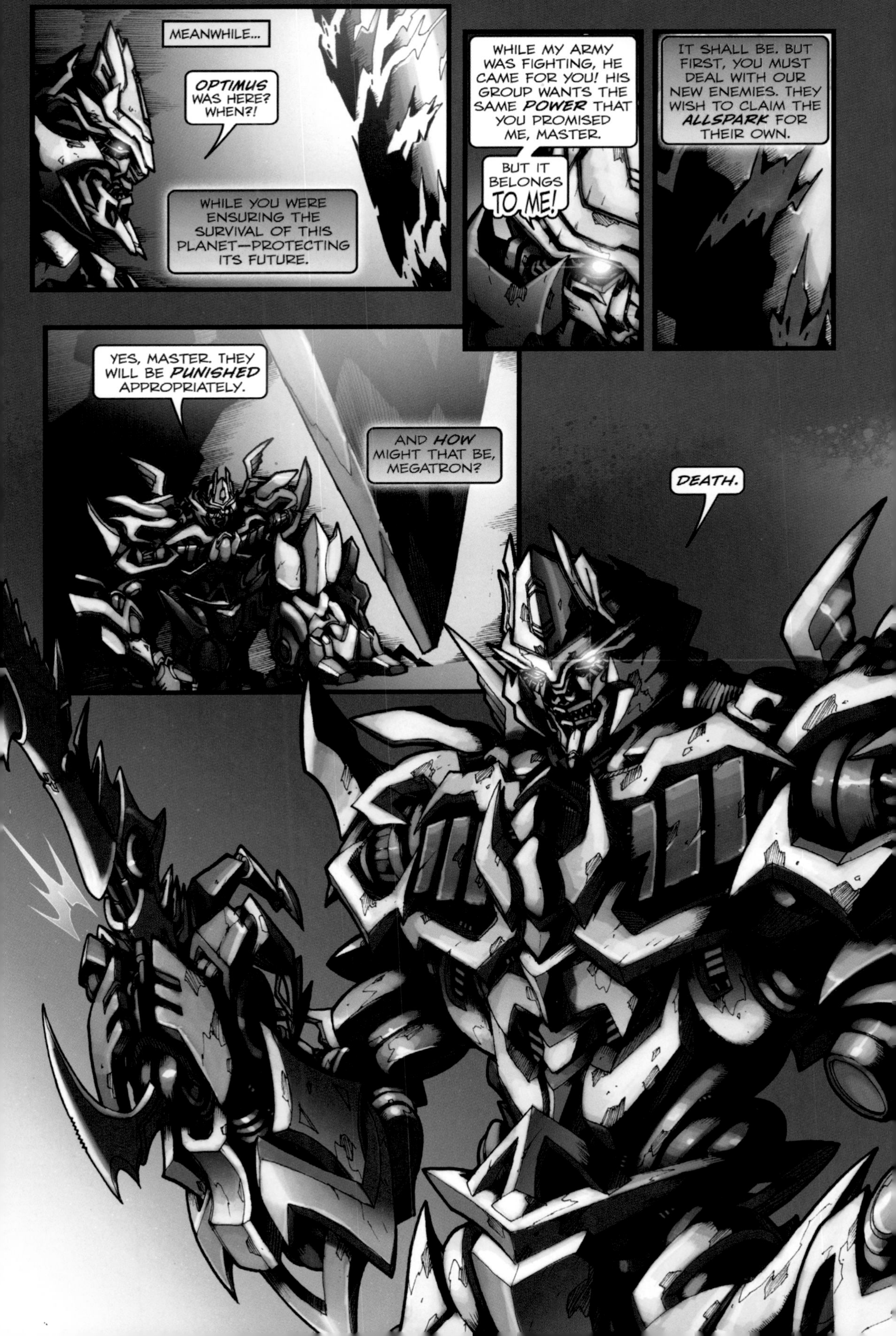

MEANWHILE...
OPTIMUS WAS HERE? WHEN?!
WHILE YOU WERE ENSURING THE SURVIVAL OF THIS PLANET—PROTECTING ITS FUTURE.
WHILE MY ARMY WAS FIGHTING, HE CAME FOR YOU! HIS GROUP WANTS THE SAME POWER THAT YOU PROMISED ME, MASTER.
BUT IT BELONGS TO ME!
IT SHALL BE. BUT FIRST, YOU MUST DEAL WITH OUR NEW ENEMIES. THEY WISH TO CLAIM THE ALLSPARK FOR THEIR OWN.
YES, MASTER. THEY WILL BE PUNISHED APPROPRIATELY.
AND HOW MIGHT THAT BE, MEGATRON?
DEATH.

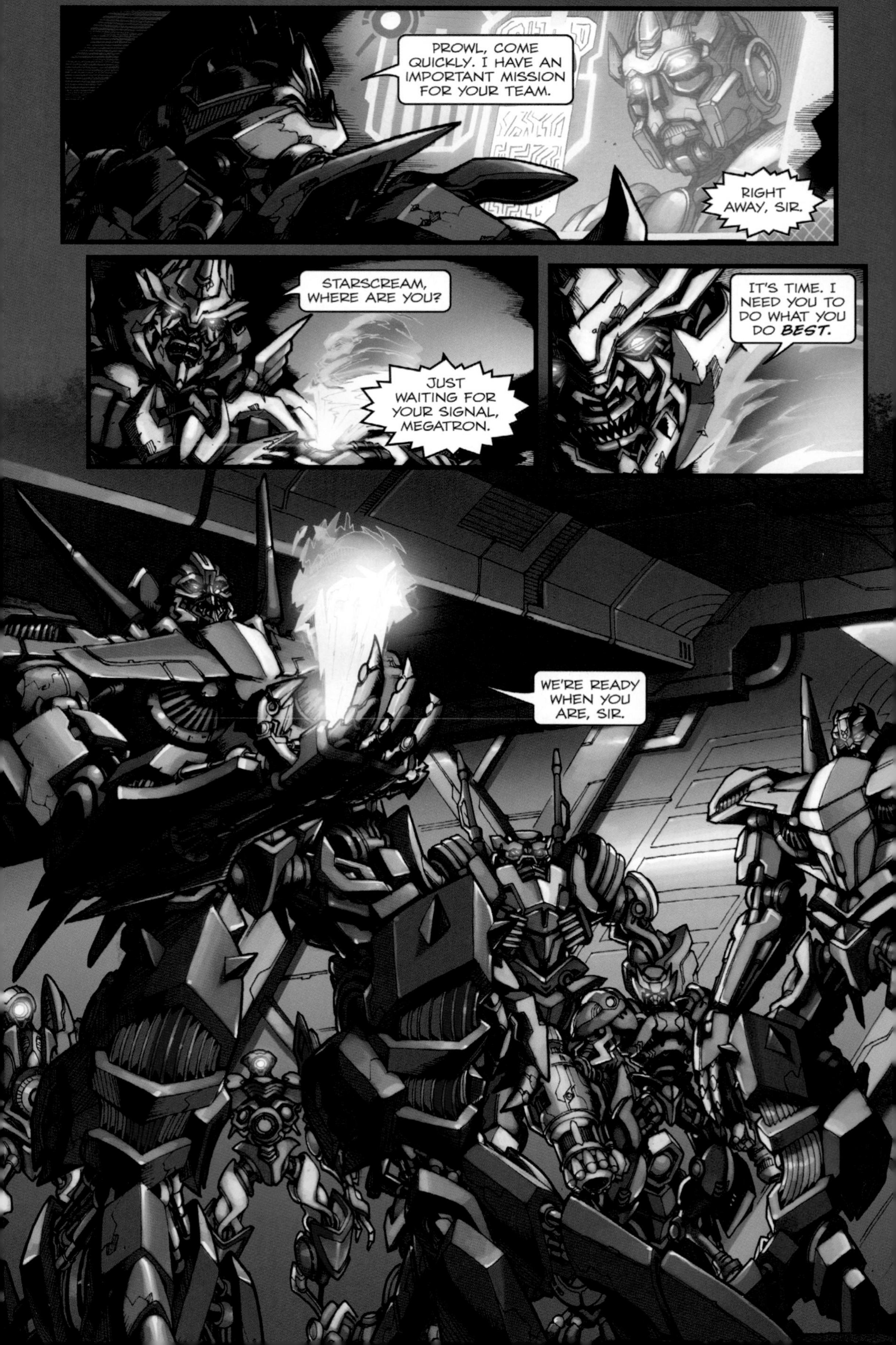
PROWL, COME QUICKLY. I HAVE AN IMPORTANT MISSION FOR YOUR TEAM.
RIGHT AWAY, SIR.
STARSCREAM, WHERE ARE YOU?
JUST WAITING FOR YOUR SIGNAL, MEGATRON.
IT'S TIME. I NEED YOU TO DO WHAT YOU DO BEST.
WE'RE READY WHEN YOU ARE, SIR.

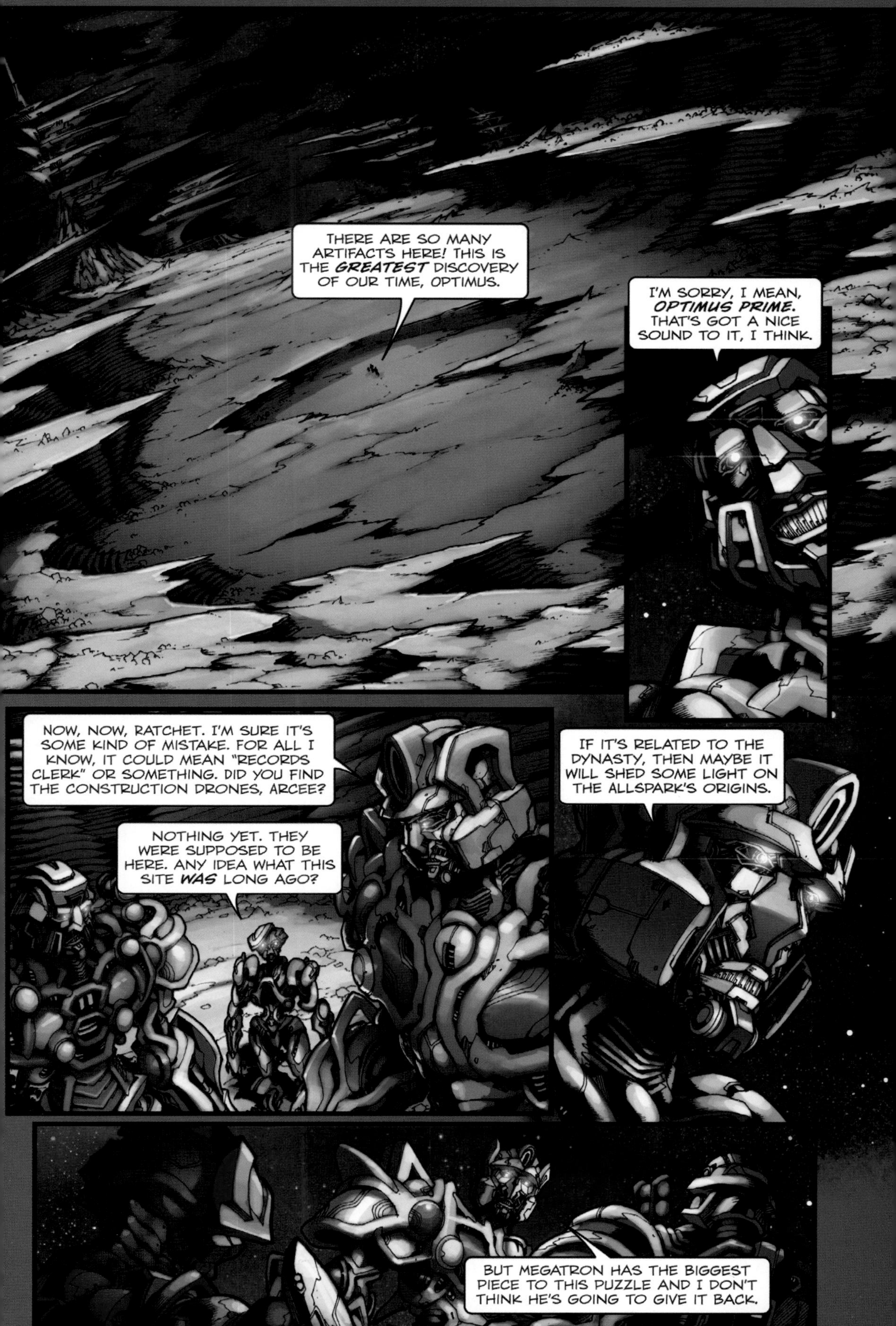
THERE ARE SO MANY ARTIFACTS HERE! THIS IS THE GREATEST DISCOVERY OF OUR TIME, OPTIMUS.
I'M SORRY, I MEAN, OPTIMUS PRIME. THAT'S GOT A NICE SOUND TO IT, I THINK.
NOW, NOW, RATCHET. I'M SURE IT'S SOME KIND OF MISTAKE. FOR ALL I KNOW, IT COULD MEAN "RECORDS CLERK" OR SOMETHING. DID YOU FIND THE CONSTRUCTION DRONES, ARCEE?
NOTHING YET. THEY WERE SUPPOSED TO BE HERE. ANY IDEA WHAT THIS SITE WAS LONG AGO?
IF IT'S RELATED TO THE DYNASTY, THEN MAYBE IT WILL SHED SOME LIGHT ON THE ALLSPARK'S ORIGINS.
BUT MEGATRON HAS THE BIGGEST PIECE TO THIS PUZZLE AND I DON'T THINK HE'S GOING TO GIVE IT BACK.

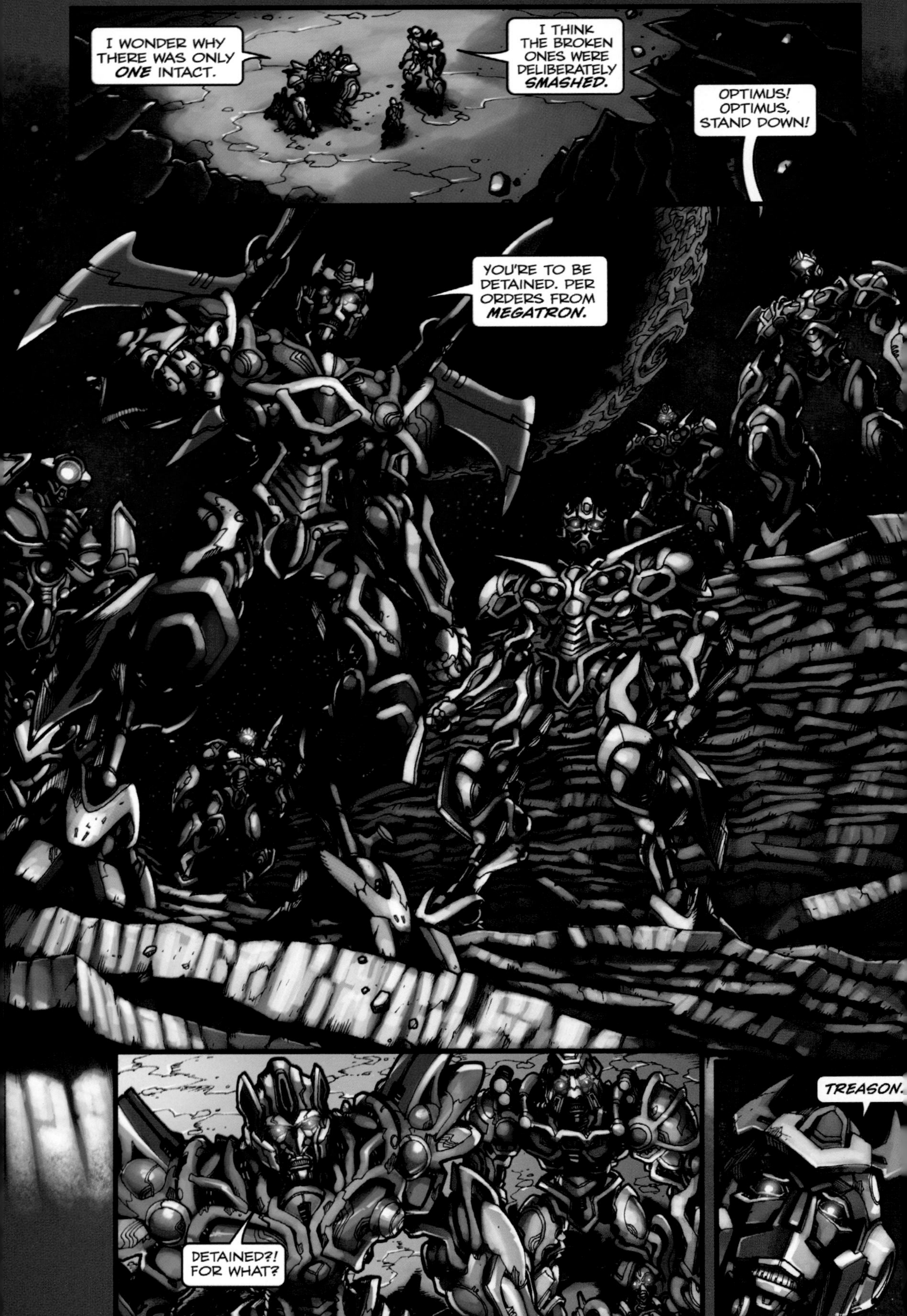
I WONDER WHY THERE WAS ONLY *ONE* INTACT.
I THINK THE BROKEN ONES WERE DELIBERATELY ***SMASHED.***
OPTIMUS! OPTIMUS, STAND DOWN!
YOU'RE TO BE DETAINED. PER ORDERS FROM ***MEGATRON.***
DETAINED?! FOR WHAT?
TREASON.

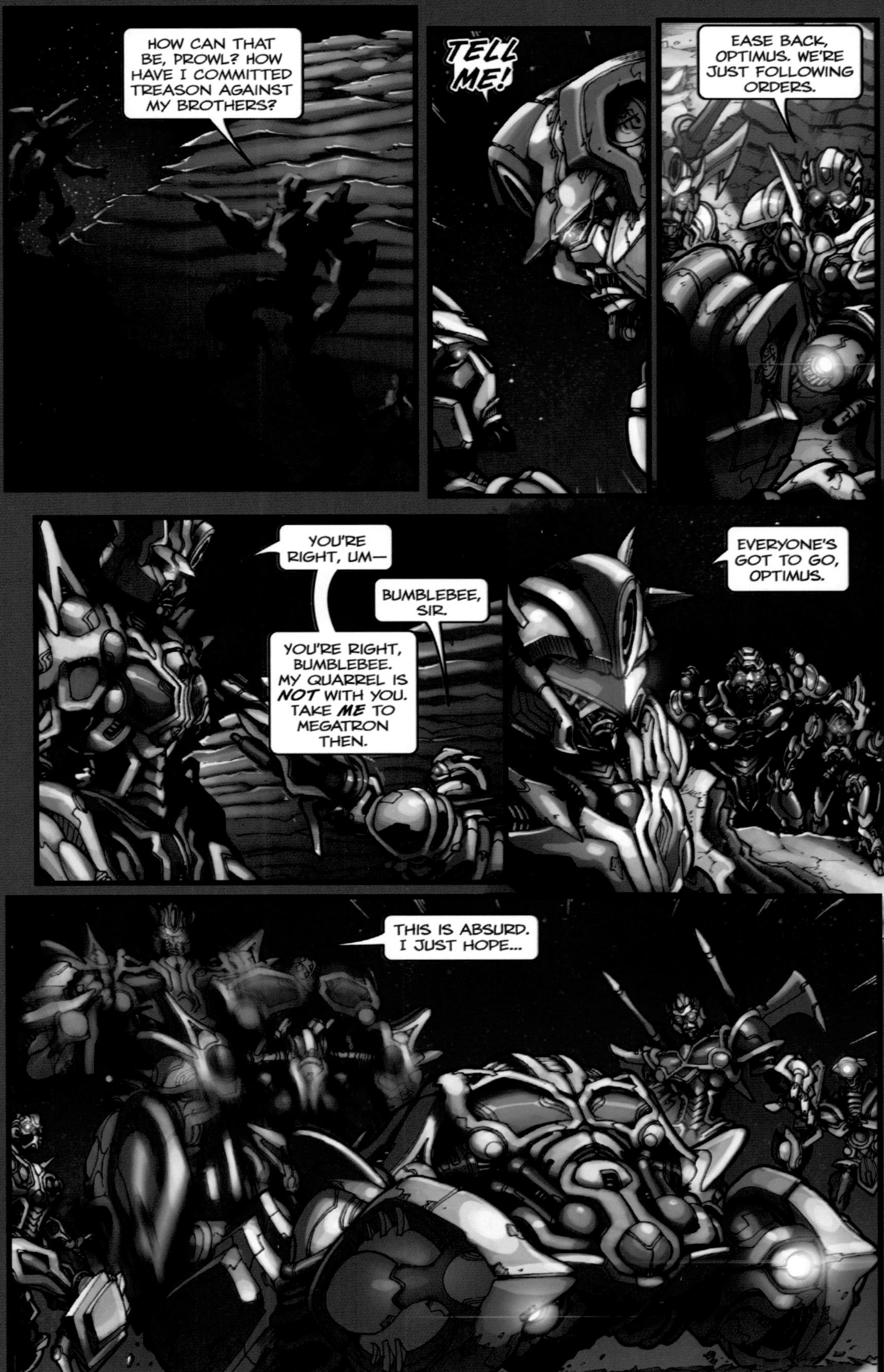
HOW CAN THAT BE, PROWL? HOW HAVE I COMMITTED TREASON AGAINST MY BROTHERS?
TELL ME!
EASE BACK, OPTIMUS. WE'RE JUST FOLLOWING ORDERS.
YOU'RE RIGHT, UM—
BUMBLEBEE, SIR.
YOU'RE RIGHT, BUMBLEBEE. MY QUARREL IS NOT WITH YOU. TAKE ME TO MEGATRON THEN.
EVERYONE'S GOT TO GO, OPTIMUS.
THIS IS ABSURD. I JUST HOPE...

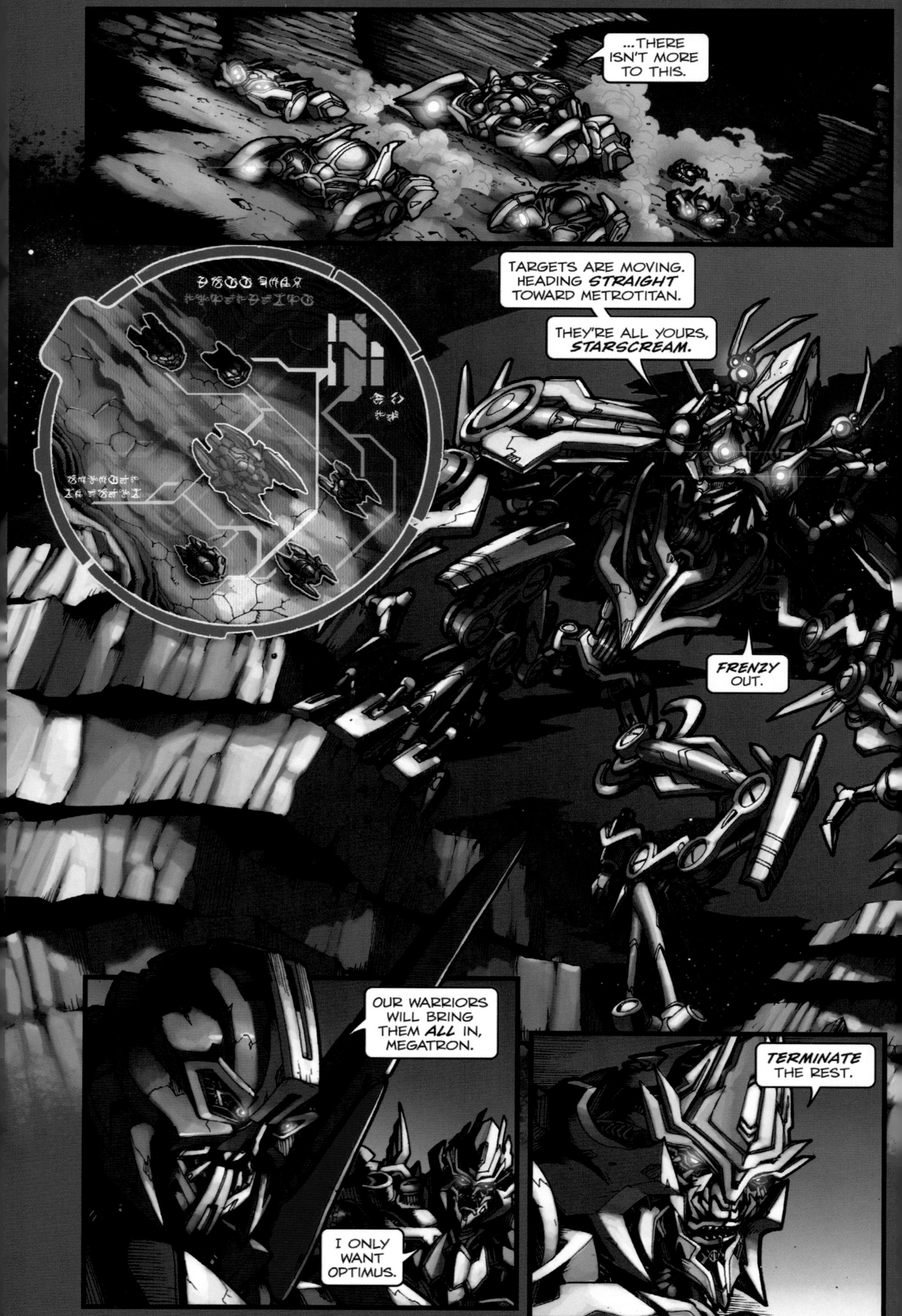
...THERE ISN'T MORE TO THIS.
TARGETS ARE MOVING. HEADING STRAIGHT TOWARD METROTITAN.
THEY'RE ALL YOURS, STARSCREAM.
FRENZY OUT.
OUR WARRIORS WILL BRING THEM ALL IN, MEGATRON.
I ONLY WANT OPTIMUS.
TERMINATE THE REST.

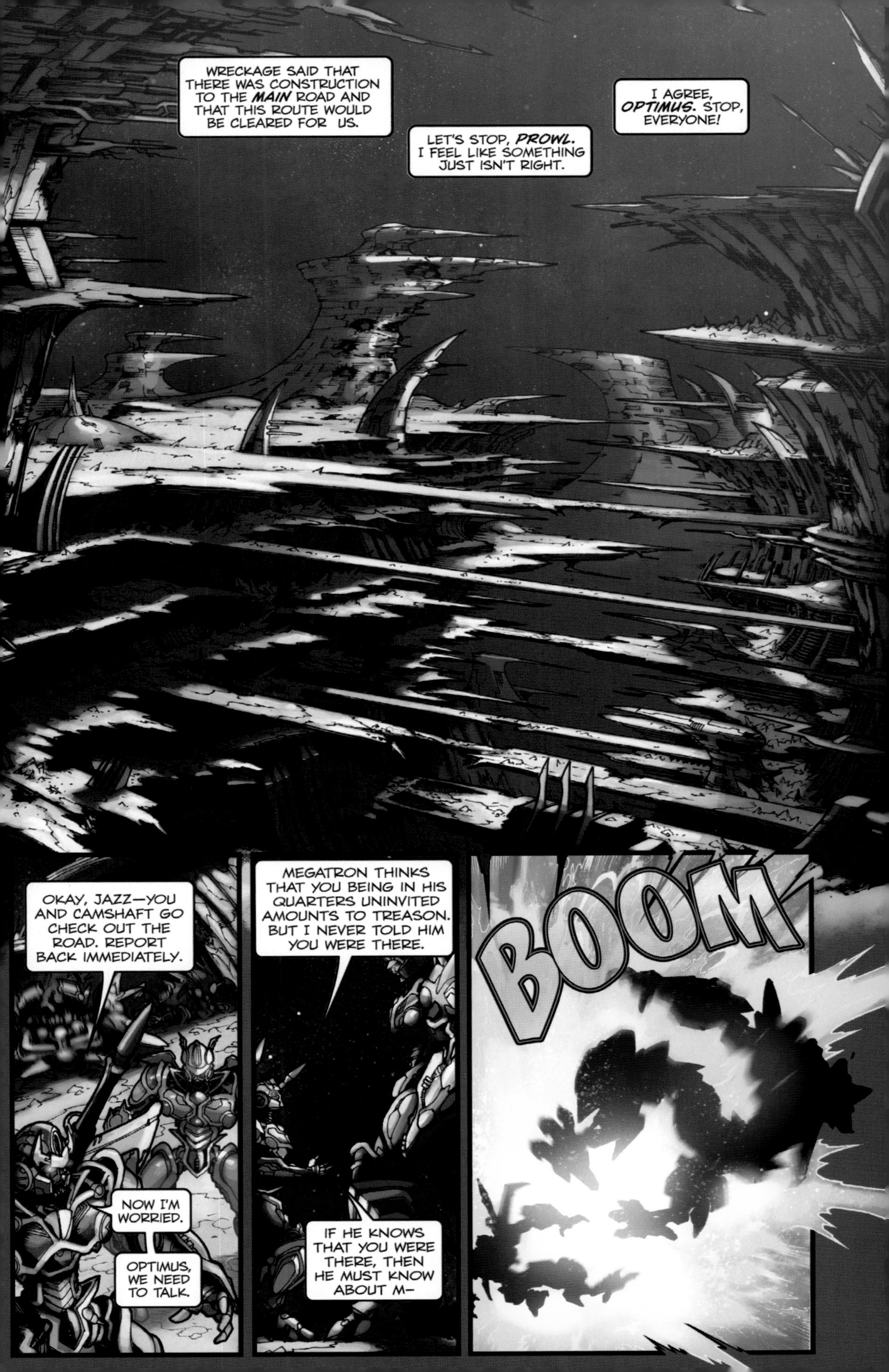

WRECKAGE SAID THAT THERE WAS CONSTRUCTION TO THE MAIN ROAD AND THAT THIS ROUTE WOULD BE CLEARED FOR US.
LET'S STOP, PROWL. I FEEL LIKE SOMETHING JUST ISN'T RIGHT.
I AGREE, OPTIMUS. STOP, EVERYONE!
OKAY, JAZZ—YOU AND CAMSHAFT GO CHECK OUT THE ROAD. REPORT BACK IMMEDIATELY.
NOW I'M WORRIED.
OPTIMUS, WE NEED TO TALK.
MEGATRON THINKS THAT YOU BEING IN HIS QUARTERS UNINVITED AMOUNTS TO TREASON. BUT I NEVER TOLD HIM YOU WERE THERE.
IF HE KNOWS THAT YOU WERE THERE, THEN HE MUST KNOW ABOUT M—
BOOM

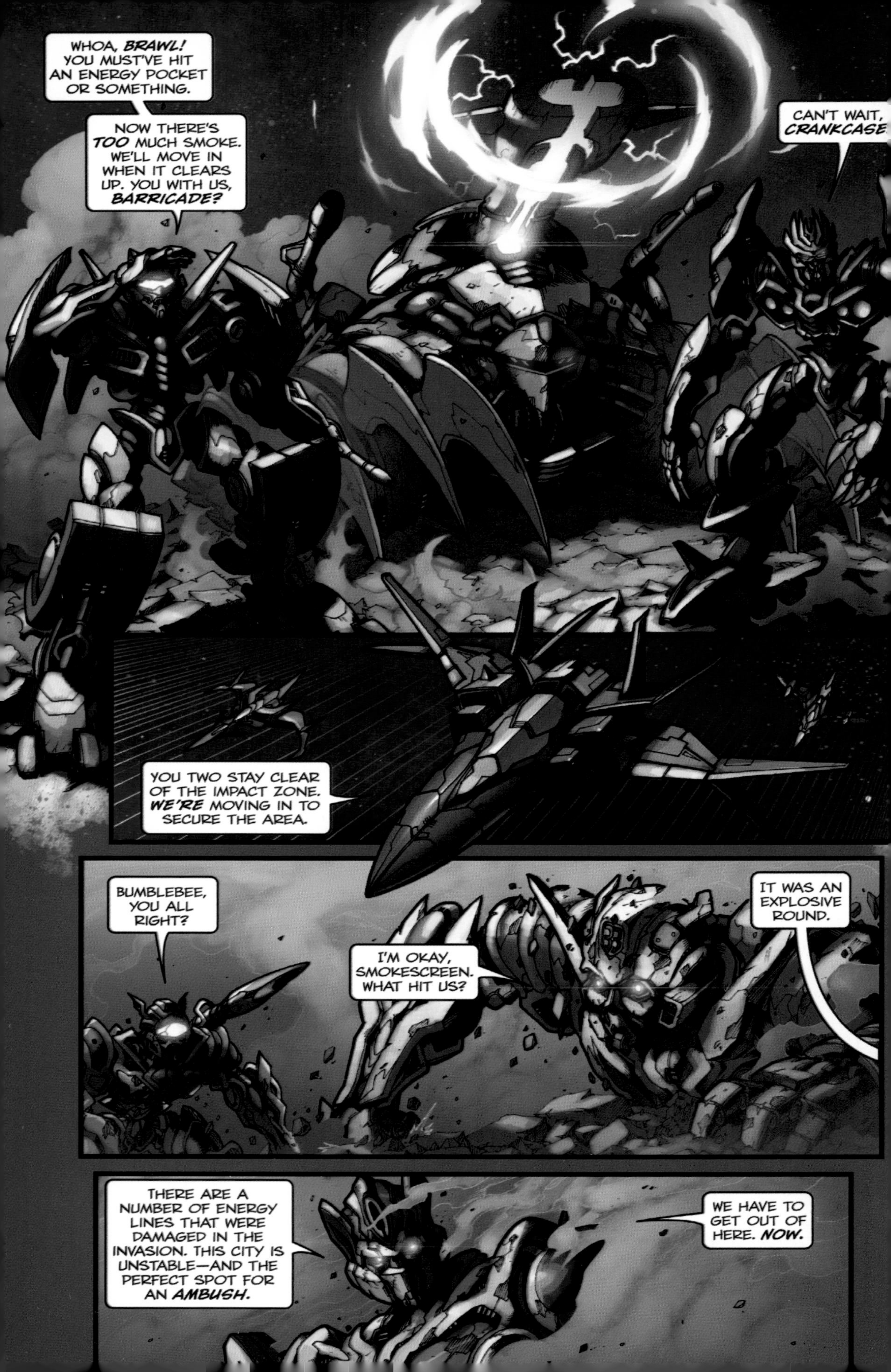

WHOA, BRAWL! YOU MUST'VE HIT AN ENERGY POCKET OR SOMETHING.
NOW THERE'S TOO MUCH SMOKE. WE'LL MOVE IN WHEN IT CLEARS UP. YOU WITH US, BARRICADE?
CAN'T WAIT, CRANKCASE.
YOU TWO STAY CLEAR OF THE IMPACT ZONE. WE'RE MOVING IN TO SECURE THE AREA.
BUMBLEBEE, YOU ALL RIGHT?
I'M OKAY, SMOKESCREEN. WHAT HIT US?
IT WAS AN EXPLOSIVE ROUND.
THERE ARE A NUMBER OF ENERGY LINES THAT WERE DAMAGED IN THE INVASION. THIS CITY IS UNSTABLE—AND THE PERFECT SPOT FOR AN AMBUSH.
WE HAVE TO GET OUT OF HERE. NOW.

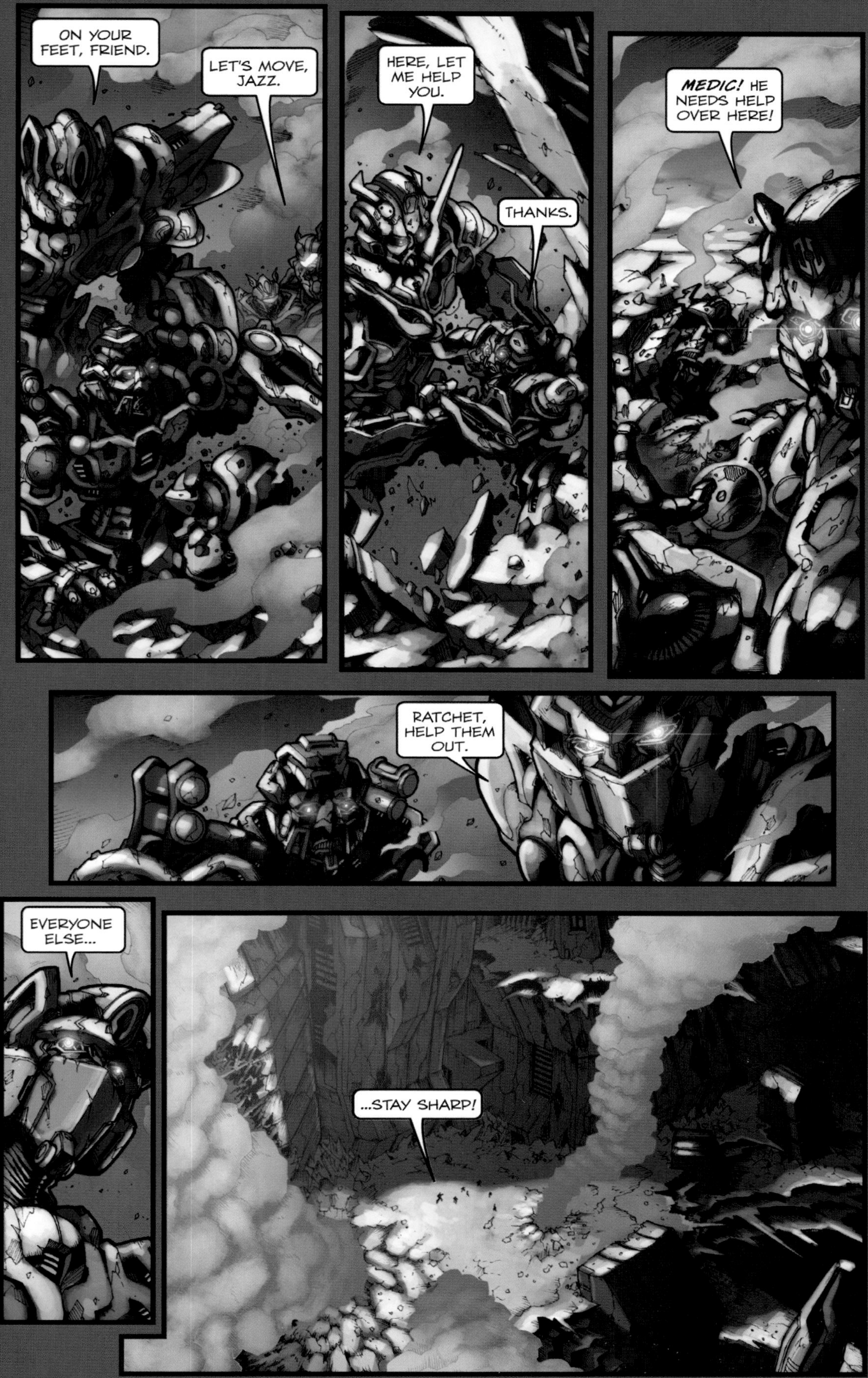
ON YOUR FEET, FRIEND.
LET'S MOVE, JAZZ.
HERE, LET ME HELP YOU.
THANKS.
MEDIC! HE NEEDS HELP OVER HERE!
RATCHET, HELP THEM OUT.
EVERYONE ELSE...
...STAY SHARP!

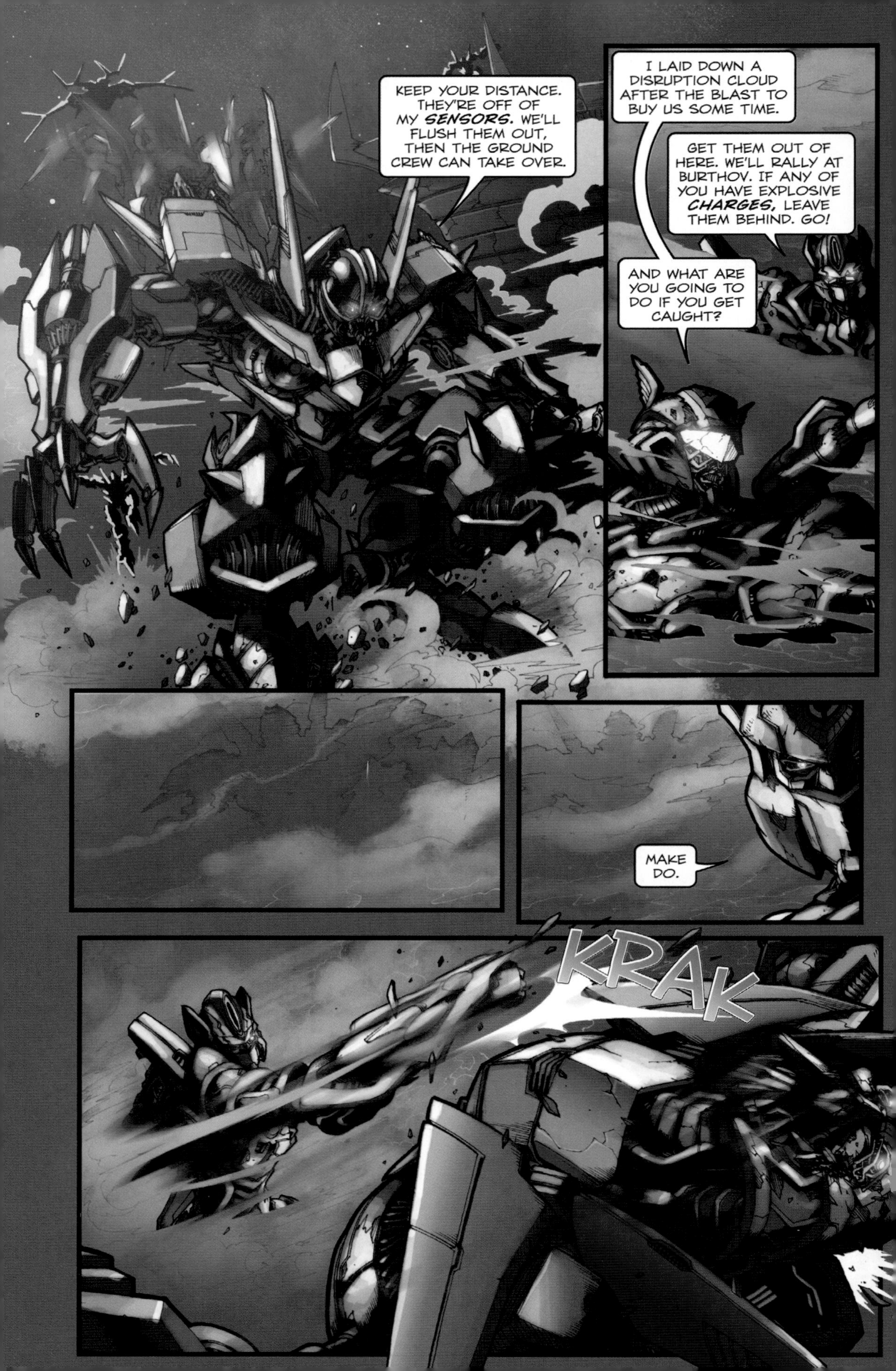
KEEP YOUR DISTANCE. THEY'RE OFF OF MY SENSORS. WE'LL FLUSH THEM OUT, THEN THE GROUND CREW CAN TAKE OVER.
I LAID DOWN A DISRUPTION CLOUD AFTER THE BLAST TO BUY US SOME TIME.
GET THEM OUT OF HERE. WE'LL RALLY AT BURTHOV. IF ANY OF YOU HAVE EXPLOSIVE CHARGES, LEAVE THEM BEHIND. GO!
AND WHAT ARE YOU GOING TO DO IF YOU GET CAUGHT?
MAKE DO.
KRAK

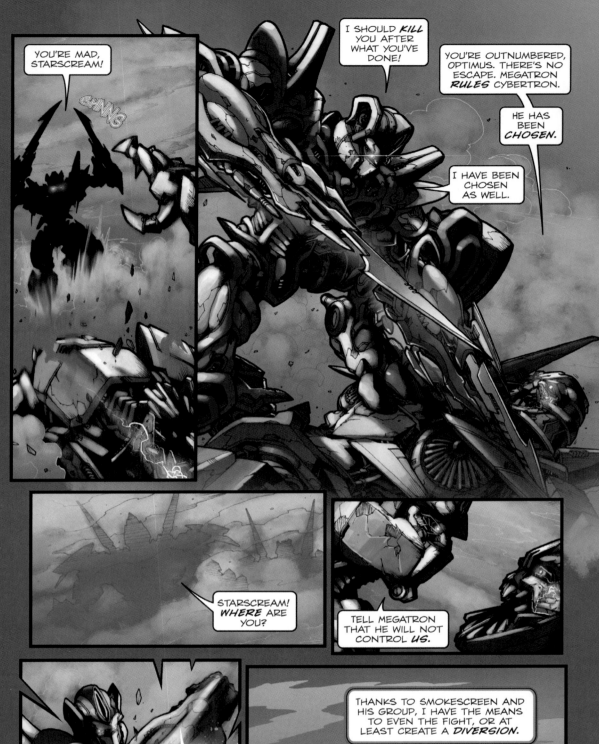

YOU'RE MAD, STARSCREAM!

SHNNG

I SHOULD *KILL* YOU AFTER WHAT YOU'VE DONE!

YOU'RE OUTNUMBERED, OPTIMUS. THERE'S NO ESCAPE. MEGATRON *RULES* CYBERTRON.

HE HAS BEEN *CHOSEN*.

I HAVE BEEN CHOSEN AS WELL.

STARSCREAM! *WHERE* ARE YOU?

TELL MEGATRON THAT HE WILL NOT CONTROL *US*.

WHAK

THANKS TO SMOKESCREEN AND HIS GROUP, I HAVE THE MEANS TO EVEN THE FIGHT, OR AT LEAST CREATE A *DIVERSION*.

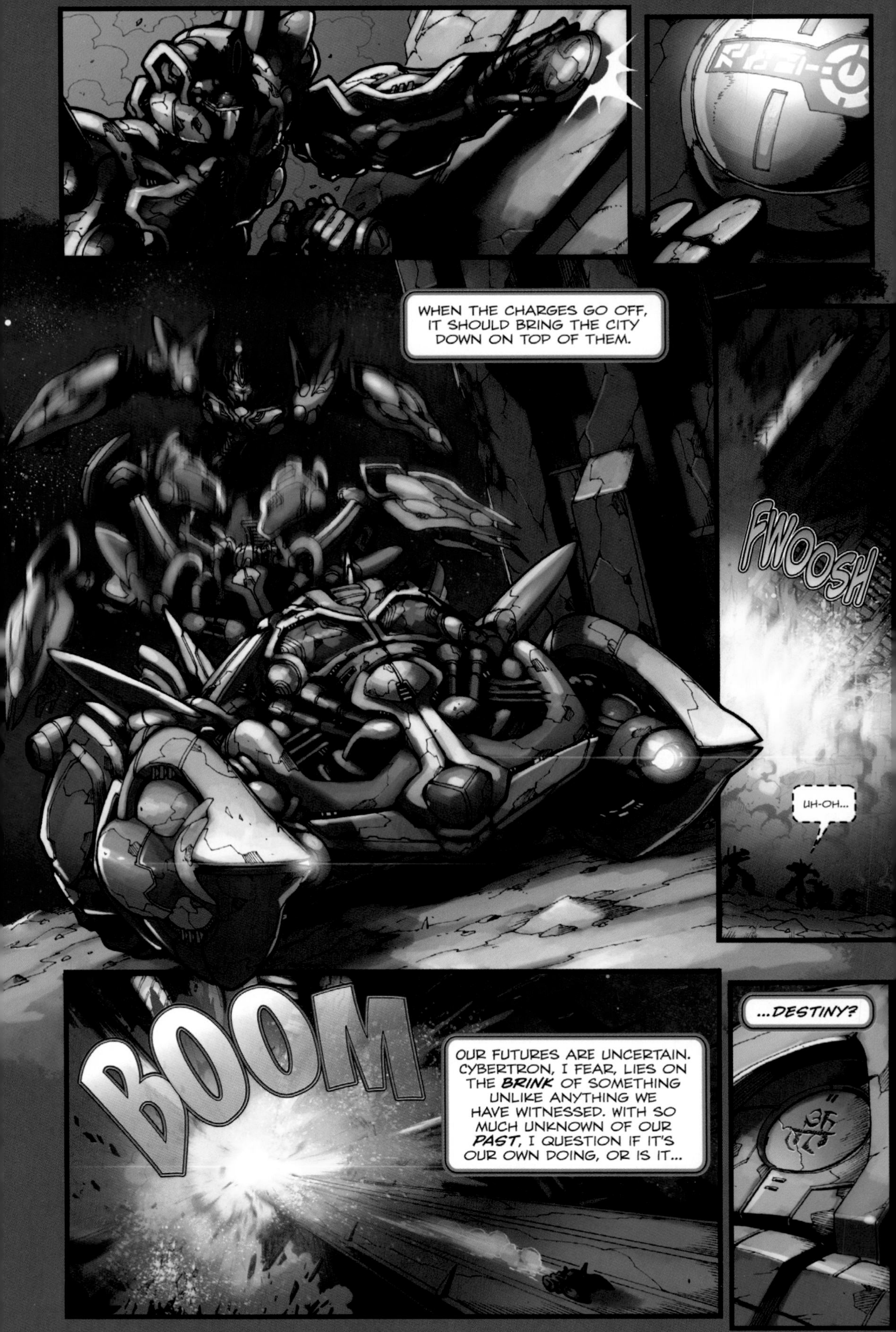
WHEN THE CHARGES GO OFF, IT SHOULD BRING THE CITY DOWN ON TOP OF THEM.
FWOOSH
UH-OH...
BOOM
OUR FUTURES ARE UNCERTAIN. CYBERTRON, I FEAR, LIES ON THE BRINK OF SOMETHING UNLIKE ANYTHING WE HAVE WITNESSED. WITH SO MUCH UNKNOWN OF OUR PAST, I QUESTION IF IT'S OUR OWN DOING, OR IS IT...
...DESTINY?

LATER IN TRYPTICON.

MY WARRIORS OF CYBERTRON. WE HAVE REMAINED *PEACEFUL* FOR TOO LONG. WHERE HAS THE PATH OF CIVILITY BROUGHT US?

ATTACKS FROM BEYOND OUR PLANET—AND FROM OUR OWN KIND. BETRAYED BY OUR OWN BROTHERS!

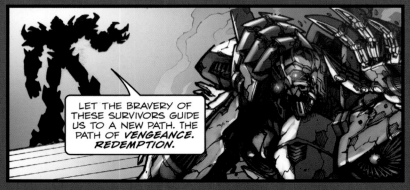

LET THE BRAVERY OF THESE SURVIVORS GUIDE US TO A NEW PATH. THE PATH OF *VENGEANCE. REDEMPTION.*

DEFIANCE!

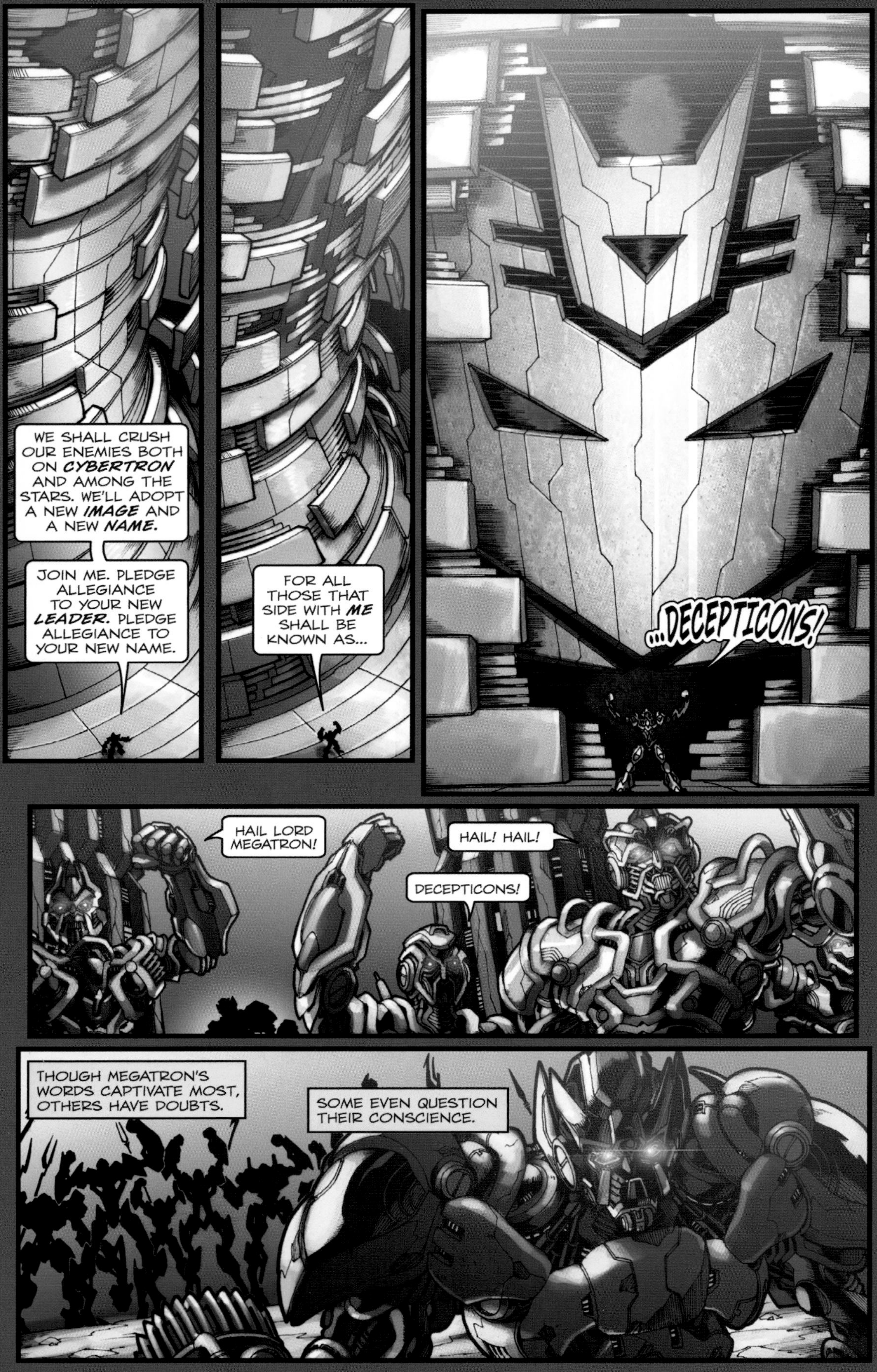
WE SHALL CRUSH OUR ENEMIES BOTH ON CYBERTRON AND AMONG THE STARS. WE'LL ADOPT A NEW IMAGE AND A NEW NAME.
JOIN ME. PLEDGE ALLEGIANCE TO YOUR NEW LEADER. PLEDGE ALLEGIANCE TO YOUR NEW NAME.
FOR ALL THOSE THAT SIDE WITH ME SHALL BE KNOWN AS...
...DECEPTICONS!
HAIL LORD MEGATRON!
HAIL! HAIL!
DECEPTICONS!
THOUGH MEGATRON'S WORDS CAPTIVATE MOST, OTHERS HAVE DOUBTS.
SOME EVEN QUESTION THEIR CONSCIENCE.